STANLEY, FLAT AGAIN!

by Jeff Brown

Pictures by Scott Nash

EGMONT

**Read all of
Stanley Lambchop's adventures
by Jeff Brown**

Flat Stanley
Stanley and the Magic Lamp
Invisible Stanley
Stanley in Space
Stanley's Christmas Adventure
Stanley, Flat Again!

CONTENTS

1. A Morning Surprise 1

2. Dr Stan 13

3. Stanley Sails 21

4. Back to School 35

5. Why Me? 45

6. Emma 53

7. Where Are You, Emma? 63

8. Hero! 77

9. Fame! 83

DAILY SENTINEL

SUPER CHICKEN!

SWEDES
BREED
PEDDLING
POULTRY

...RE FORCE

Chapter One

A Morning Surprise

Mrs Lambchop was making breakfast. Mr Lambchop, at the kitchen table, helped by reading bits from the morning paper.

'Here's an odd one, Harriet,' he said. 'There's a chicken in Sweden that rides a bike.'

'So do I, George,' said Mrs Lambchop, not really listening.

'Listen to this. "Merker Building now empty. To be collapsed next week." Imagine! Eight floors!'

'Poor thing!' Mrs Lambchop set out plates. 'My, isn't this a lovely sunny morning!' She raised her voice. 'Boys! Breakfast is ready!'

Her glance fell upon a row of
photographs on the wall above the sink.
There was a smiling Stanley, only half an
inch thick, his big bulletin board having
fallen from the bedroom wall to rest upon
him overnight. Next came reminders of
the many family adventures that had come

after Stanley's younger brother, Arthur, had cleverly blown him round again with a bicycle pump. There were the brothers with Prince Haraz, the young genie who had granted wishes for them all after being accidentally summoned by Stanley from a lamp. There was the entire family with Santa Claus and his daughter, Sarah, taken during a Christmas visit to the North Pole. There was the family again in Washington DC, in the office of the President of the United States, who had asked them to undertake a secret mission into outer space. The last picture showed Arthur standing beside a balloon on which Mrs Lambchop had painted a picture of Stanley's face. The balloon, its string in fact held by Stanley, had been a valuable guide to his presence, since he was invisible at the time. 'Boys!' she called again. 'Breakfast!'

In their bedroom, Stanley and Arthur had finished dressing.

While Stanley filled his backpack, Arthur bounced a tennis ball. 'Let's go,' he said. 'Here! Catch!'

Stanley had just reached for a book on the shelf by his bed. The ball struck his back as he turned, and he banged his shoulder on a corner of the shelf.

'Ouch!'

'Sorry,' Arthur said. 'But let's go, okay? You know how long – STANLEY!'

'Why are you shouting?' Stanley adjusted

his pack. 'C'mon! I'm so hungry –' He paused. 'Oh, boy! Arthur, do you see?'

'I do, actually.' Arthur swallowed hard. 'You're, you know . . . flat.'

The brothers stared at each other.

'The pump?' Stanley said. 'It might work again.'

Arthur fetched the bicycle pump from their toy chest and Stanley lay on the bed with the hose end in his mouth.

Arthur gave a long, steady, pump.

Stanley made a face. 'That hurts!'

Arthur pumped again, and Stanley snatched the hose from his mouth. 'Owww! That really hurts! It wasn't like that before. We'd better stop.'

'Now what?' Arthur said. 'We can't just

hide in here forever, you know.'

Mrs Lambchop's call came again. 'Boys! Please come!'

'Do me a favour,' Stanley said. 'You tell them. Sort of get them ready, okay?'

'Okay,' said Arthur, and went to tell.

Arthur stood in the kitchen doorway.

'Hey, guess what?' he said.

'Hay is for horses, dear,' said Mrs Lambchop. 'Good morning! Breakfast is ready.'

'School, Arthur,' Mr Lambchop said from behind his newspaper. 'Where's Stanley?'

'Guess what?' Arthur said again.

Mrs Lambchop sighed. 'Oh, all right! I can't guess. Tell.'

'Stanley's flat again,' said Arthur.

Mr Lambchop put down his paper.

Mrs Lambchop closed her eyes. 'Flat again? Is that what you said?'

'Yes,' said Arthur.

'It's true.' Stanley stood now beside Arthur in the doorway. 'Just look.'

'Good grief!' said Mr Lambchop. 'I can't

believe that bulletin board –'

'It didn't fall on me this time,' Stanley said. 'I just got flat. Arthur tried to pump me up, like before, but it hurt too much.'

'Oh, Stanley!' Mrs Lambchop ran to kiss him. 'How do you feel now?'

'Fine, actually,' Stanley said. 'Just surprised. Can I go to school?'

Mrs Lambchop thought for a moment. 'Very well. Eat your breakfast. After school we'll hear what Dr Dan has to say.'

Chapter Two

Dr Dan

'Ah, Mr and Mrs Lambchop! And the boys!' said Dr Dan as they entered his office. 'How nice to –'

His eyes widened. 'Good heavens, Stanley! Mr Lambchop, you really must do something about that bulletin board!'

'It is still firmly in place, Dr Dan,' Mrs Lambchop said. 'We are at a loss to account for this attack of flatness.'

'Hmm.' Dr Dan thought for a moment. 'Is there, perhaps, a family history of flatness?'

'No,' Mr Lambchop said. 'We'd remember that.'

'We got dressed for school,' Stanley explained. 'We didn't even have breakfast. And all of a sudden, I got flat.'

Dr Dan frowned. 'Nothing happened? Nothing at all?'

'Well, Arthur hit me with a tennis ball,' Stanley said. 'And then I banged my shoulder on –'

'Aha!' Jumping up, Dr Dan took a large book from the case behind his desk and began turning pages. 'This is Dr Franz

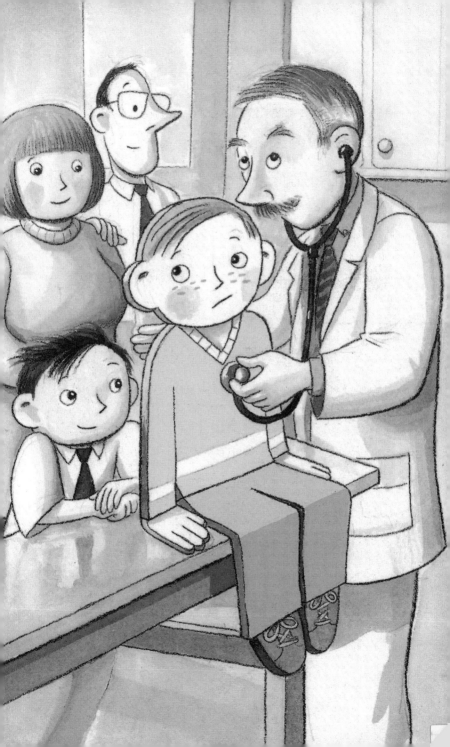

Gemeister's excellent *Difficult and Peculiar Cases*. Just let me find . . . Here it is! "Flatness", page 217!'

He read aloud. ' "Sudden flatness . . . extremely rare . . . minimal documentation . . . hearsay reports . . ." Ah, here it is! ". . . account dating back to mid-fifth century AD. During battle, Mongo the

Fierce, an aide to Attila the Hun, was struck twice, simultaneously, from behind, and at once became no thicker than his shield. He became known as Mongo the Plate, and lived to old age without regaining his original girth."'

Dr Dan closed the book. 'As I suspected! The OBP.'

'Beg pardon?' said Mrs Lambchop.

'The OBP. Osteal Balance Point,' Dr Dan explained. 'A little-known anatomical feature. The human body, of course, is a complex miracle, its skeleton a delicate framework of supports and balances. The Osteal Balance Point may occur almost anywhere in the upper torso. It is vulnerable only to the application of simultaneous pressures at two points which vary depending on the age and particular "design", let us say, of the individual involved. In my opinion, the pressures created by the tennis ball and the shelf corner affected Stanley's OBP, thereby turning him flat.'

For a moment, everyone was silent.

'The first time Stanley went flat, you were greatly puzzled by his condition,' Mr Lambchop said at last. 'Now you seem remarkably well informed.'

'I read up on it,' said Dr Dan.

Mrs Lambchop sighed. 'Perhaps we should seek a second opinion. Who is the world's leading authority on the OBP?'

'That would be me,' said Dr Dan.

'I see . . . Well, we've taken enough of your time.' Mr Lambchop rose, motioning his family to follow. 'Thank you, Dr Dan.'

At the door, Mrs Lambchop turned. 'Perhaps if we found the, you know, the OBP, we could make Stanley –'

'No, no!' said Dr Dan. 'It would be dangerous to put the lad through such a skeletal strain again! And finding the OBP? Not very likely, I'm afraid.'

Arthur had an idea. 'I know! If we all got sticks and hit Stanley all over at the same time, and kept doing it, then –'

'That will do, Arthur,' Mr Lambchop said, and led his family out.

Chapter Three

Stanley Sails

Early the next Sunday morning, Mr Lambchop had a call from an old college friend, Ralph Jones.

'Just wanted to remind you, George, that Stanley and I have a date to go sailing today,' he said.

'He's looking forward to it, Ralph.' Mr Lambchop hesitated. 'I should mention, perhaps, that Stanley has gone flat again.'

Mr Jones sighed. 'I thought he'd got over that. Well, I'll pick him up at ten.'

Later that morning, driving with Stanley to his sailing club on the seashore, Mr Jones inquired about a foreign visitor he had once met with the Lambchops. 'A prince, yes? He around these days?'

Stanley knew he meant the young genie, Prince Haraz, but it would be difficult to explain not only the genie part, but also that Haraz had returned to the genie kingdom from which he had come.

'No,' Stanley said. 'He went home, actually.'

'Too bad.' Mr Jones was famous for his amazing memory. 'Haraz, as I recall.

Prince Fawzi Mustafa Aslan Mirza Malek Namerd Haraz?'

'Right,' said Stanley.

In the harbour of the sailing club, Mr Jones prepared his boat, *Lovebug*, and explained it to Stanley. 'This big sail here is the mainsail, and that's the rudder back there, for steering. In this zip bag is another sail, called a spinnaker. We'll use that one for extra speed when we're running before the wind. See that boat way out there, how its spinnaker is puffing out front?'

Stanley laughed. The spinnaker looked like an open umbrella lying on its side.

'See over there,' Mr Jones went on, 'between the committee boat, with the judges on it, and the red buoy? That's the starting line. The race ends back there too. First boat to cross that line wins!'

He cast off the mooring line, and the mainsail filled. *Lovebug* headed out to join the other boats.

Mr Jones pointed. 'There! That's Jasper Green's boat, *Windswept*. He's the one I want especially to beat!'

'Why? Are you mad at him?' Stanley asked.

'He was very rude to me once. But never mind. Let's just make sure we win!'

Behind the start line, they found themselves beside *Windswept*. Jasper Green gave a friendly wave, but Ralph Jones ignored him.

'You're always in a bad mood with me, Ralph,' Mr Green said. 'Why? I don't – Here we go!'

A pistol shot had signalled the start of the race. *Lovebug* and *Windswept* and the other racers glided across the start line behind the motor-powered committee boat, which led them along a course marked by buoys with bright green streamers.

Stanley sat back, enjoying himself. The sun was bright, the breeze fresh against his face, the sky clear and blue, the water a beautiful slate colour. There were boats on both sides of them, boats ahead, boats behind. How pretty they were, their white sails making cheerful crackling sounds as they billowed in the wind!

Along the shore, people waved from the porches of houses, their voices carrying faintly on the wind. 'Way to go! . . . Looking good, sailors! . . . Looking flat, one of them!' Stanley waved back, knowing that the teasing was kindly meant.

Lovebug passed other boats, but there

were many more still ahead. And now they were almost abreast of *Windswept*. Stanley saw that Jasper Green had hoisted his spinnaker, and that other boats had too.

'I've got you beat, Ralph!' Jasper Green shouted.

'We'll just round this point, Stanley! Then – Now!' exclaimed Ralph Jones. 'Let's show Jasper what running before the wind really means!'

He attached his spinnaker to a halyard and ran it up the mast. *Who-o-oosh*! The spinnaker billowed out, and Stanley felt *Lovebug* surge forward, as if pushed by an invisible hand.

'Here we go!' shouted Ralph Jones.

They passed five more boats, three more,

then *Windswept*! They were ahead of everyone now, and the finish line lay ahead!

'We're going to win!' Stanley shouted.

'Yes!' Ralph Jones shouted back. 'Just wait till Jasper —'

R-i-i-i-i-p!

The sound came from above. Looking up, they saw that the top of the spinnaker had torn.

R-i-i-i-i-i-i-i-p!

The rip streaked downward, and now the spinnaker, torn all the way down, flapped uselessly in the wind. *Lovebug* slowed.

'Drat!' Mr Jones did his best with the mainsail. 'Drat, drat, drat!'

Windswept came up behind them.

'Tough luck!' called Jasper Green. 'Ha, ha!'

'Drat!' Mr Jones sighed. 'Nothing we can do, Stanley. Unless . . . This may be crazy, but . . . Stanley, perhaps you could be our spinnaker?'

'What?' Stanley shouted. 'How?'

'Good question,' said Mr Jones. 'Let's see . . . First go take hold of the mast. Now maybe –'

'Excuse me,' Stanley said. 'But did you ever do this before?'

'Stanley, *nobody* ever did this before.' Mr Jones took a deep breath. 'Okay. Now twist around to face forward, and grab the mast behind you above your head!'

Stanley did as he was told, planting his feet on the sides of the boat to hold him in place. The wind pressed him from behind, driving *Lovebug* toward the finish line.

'Yes! Chest forward! Butt back!' shouted Mr Jones. 'Best spinnaker I ever had!' In a moment they had passed *Windswept*, and Stanley could not help laughing at the surprise on Jasper Green's face.

And then they were across the finish line! *Lovebug* had won!

Back in the clubhouse, Jasper Green would not admit that he had lost. A flat person used as a sail? He had never seen *that* before, he said, and went to the race committee office to complain. But he returned shortly to report that *Lovebug* had indeed won. The committee had advised him, he said, that there was no rule against a crew member allowing the wind to blow against him.

'Great sailing, Ralph!' he said. 'I thought it was my race, I really did!'

'Thank you, Jasper,' Mr Jones said, but Stanley noticed that he did not smile.

Jasper Green noticed too. 'Ralph, you're still mad at me,' he said. 'But *why*?'

'You spilled coffee on my white trousers, Jasper,' said Ralph Jones. 'And you just laughed when I jumped up.'

'What?' Jasper Green seemed greatly surprised. 'I don't remember – Where? When?'

'We were having lunch,' said Mr Jones. 'At the old Vandercook Hotel.'

'The Vandercook? It closed down twenty years ago!' Mr Green slapped his forehead. 'I *do* remember! That lunch was twenty years ago, Ralph!'

'Twenty-one, actually.'

'All right, all right!' said Mr Green. 'I apologise, for heaven's sake!'

Ralph Jones smiled warmly. 'Perfectly all right, Jasper,' he said. 'Don't give it another thought.'

Chapter Four

Back to School

Back at school, Stanley was pleased that his classmates, who still remembered his previous flatness, made no great fuss about it now. Mostly they expressed only cheerful interest. 'Feeling okay, Stan?' they said, and 'Lookin' sharp, man! Sharp, see? Get the joke?' Only mean Emma Weeks was unpleasant. 'Huh! Mr Show-off again!'

Emma said one day, but Stanley pretended not to hear.

He had been back at school for a week when a newspaper, learning of this unusually shaped student, sent a photographer to investigate. He found Stanley watching a practice on the football field.

'Flash Tobin,' he said. 'From the *Daily Sentinel*. You're the flat kid, right?'

Stanley thought he must be joking. 'How did you know?' he said, joking back.

'How did I –' The photographer laughed. 'Oh, I get it! Can I take your picture, kid? Right here by the goal posts?'

Stanley nodded, and Flash Tobin took his picture. 'I heard there was a flat kid here

before,' he said. 'Helped catch sneak thieves at the Famous Museum of Art. But that kid, I heard he got round again.'

'It was me,' Stanley told him.

'You go back and forth, huh?' The photographer was impressed. 'Okay, get round now. I'd like a shot of that too.'

'I can't just do it when I want,' Stanley explained. 'The first time, my brother had to blow me up. With a bicycle pump.'

'Make a great picture!' Flash Tobin

shook his head. 'Well, we'll just go with flat.'

Stanley's picture was in the *Daily Sentinel* the next morning, and Arthur could not help showing his jealousy. Stanley was always getting his picture in the paper, he said. Didn't they see how interesting it would be to have a picture of his brother?

There was a football team practice that afternoon, and the day was windy. It was worrisome, the coach said, the way Stanley got blown about. Perhaps, for the sake of the team, he should switch to an indoor sport.

Stanley loved football, and the more he thought about what the coach had said, the sadder he felt.

Miss Elliott, his form teacher, noticed that he was not his usual cheerful self. 'Mr Redfield, the new guidance counsellor, is said to be very helpful to troubled students,' she told him. 'Shall I ask him to find a time for you?'

'I guess,' Stanley said, and Miss Elliott spoke to him again after lunch. 'Such good luck, Stanley! Mr Redfield will see you right after school today!'

'Come in, Stanley. Sit right there!' Mr Redfield pointed to a comfortable chair.

Stanley sat, and Mr Redfield leaned back behind his desk. 'Now then . . . You do understand that anything you say here is completely confidential? I won't

tell anybody.'

Stanley wondered what he could say that would interest anybody else.

'Miss Elliott tells me you seem troubled.' Mr Redfield lowered his voice. 'What's wrong?'

'I'm not sure, actually,' Stanley said.

Mr Redfield picked up a pad and a pen. 'Speak freely. Whatever comes into your head. Anything special happen lately?'

'Well, I got flat,' Stanley said.

Mr Redfield made a note on his pad. 'I do see that, yes. How did that make you feel?'

Stanley thought for a moment. 'Flat.'

'I see.' Mr Redfield nodded. 'This flatness, it's come upon you before, I'm told. Is it possible that somehow, without even admitting it to yourself, you wanted it to happen again?'

'No way!' Stanley said firmly. 'The first time, it was kind of fun for a while. Flying like a kite, and being mailed to California, things like that. But then I got, you know, tired of it. And now I might get put off the football team.'

Mr Redfield nodded again. 'You take no pleasure now in your unusual shape?'

Stanley thought for a moment. 'Well, sometimes.' He told about being a sail, and helping Ralph Jones win a race.

Mr Redfield made another note. 'I see. This dream of being a sail, have you dreamed it before?'

Stanley stared at him. 'It wasn't a . . . It

really happened! I'm just tired of being different, I guess.'

Mr Redfield pressed his fingertips together. 'Different? How do you feel different, would you say?'

Stanley wondered how Mr Redfield could be a good guidance counsellor if he had both terrible eyesight and a terrible memory.

'Well, I'm the only one in my class who's flat,' he said. 'The whole school, actually.'

'Interesting.' Mr Redfield made another note and glanced at his watch. 'I'm afraid our time is up, Stanley. Would you like to see me again? Just let Miss Elliott know.'

'Okay,' Stanley said politely, but he didn't think he would.

Chapter Five

Why Me?

Stanley had looked sad all evening, Arthur thought. At bedtime, as they lay waiting for Mr and Mrs Lambchop to come say good night, he wondered how to cheer his brother up.

It was raining hard, and he remembered suddenly the rainy evening that Stanley had snacked on raisins, and by morning had become invisible. A little-known consequence, Dr Dan had explained, of eating fruit during bad weather.

'Hear the rain, Stanley?' he said. 'Better not eat any fruit.'

'Ha, ha, ha.' Stanley sounded cross. 'Just leave me alone, okay?'

'Stanley's in a terrible mood,' Arthur told Mr and Mrs Lambchop when they came in. 'He won't even talk to me.'

'What's wrong, my boy?' Mr Lambchop asked.

'Nothing.' Stanley put his pillow over his head.

'If my picture was in the newspaper practically every day, I'd be happy,' Arthur said. 'I mean, why –'

Mrs Lambchop hushed him. 'Stanley, dear? What is troubling you?'

'Nothing. Nothing,' Stanley said from under the pillow, and sat up. 'But why me? Why am I always getting flat, or invisible, or something? Why can't it just once be someone else?'

'I wouldn't mind, actually,' Arthur said. 'Just for a while. I —'

'Hush, Arthur!' Mrs Lambchop put out the overhead light, lit a corner lamp, and sat by Stanley on his bed. Mr Lambchop sat with Arthur. The gentle patter of the rain against the windows, the glow of the little lamp, made the bedroom cozy indeed.

'I do see what you mean, Stanley,' Mr

Lambchop said at last. 'Why do these things happen to you? Your mother and I don't know the answer either. But things often happen without there seeming to be a reason, and then something else happens, and suddenly the first thing seems to have had a purpose after all.'

'Well put, George!' Mrs Lambchop squeezed Stanley's hand. 'What we do know, Stanley dear, is that we're very proud of you, and love you very much. And we understand about the flatness, and all the other unexpected happenings, how upsetting it must be.'

'It sure is!' said Stanley. 'How would you like never knowing when you might get flat? Or invisible? Maybe someday I'll wake up ten feet tall or one inch short, or with green hair, or a tail or something!'

'I know . . .' Mrs Lambchop said softly, and Mr Lambchop came and patted Stanley's shoulder. Then they kissed both boys, switched off the lamp, and went out.

Arthur spoke into the darkened room. 'Stanley?'

'I'm trying to sleep,' said Stanley. 'What?'

'I was just thinking,' Arthur said. 'If you got invisible, and then you got flat, how would they know?'

'Huh? I don't –' Stanley laughed. 'Oh, I get it! About the flatness. Good one, Arthur.'

Arthur laughed too.

'Quiet, please,' said Stanley. 'I'm trying to sleep.'

'Okay,' Arthur said, but he chuckled several times before he fell asleep.

Emma

Mr Lambchop came home early the next afternoon, full of excitement.

'Guess what?' he said. 'The old Merker Department Store? Eight floors, all emptied out, waiting to be torn down? Well, last night most of it fell down by itself!'

He switched on the TV. 'News time! Let's get the latest!'

'. . . more on the Merker Building collapse!' a newscaster was saying. 'It's just a mountain of rubble now, folks! Three workmen have been treated for minor bruises, but no other injuries are reported. The public is requested to avoid the area until —'

A young woman ran on, handed him a slip of paper, and ran off again.

'Hold on! This just in!' The newscaster read from the slip. 'Wow! A little girl is trapped under all that wreckage! Emma Weeks, daughter of local businessman Oswald Weeks!'

'Emma Weeks!' Stanley exclaimed. 'She's in my class! No wonder she wasn't at school today!'

'Emma's not hurt, it appears,' the newscaster continued. 'Firemen called to the scene can hear her calling up through chinks in the wreckage, demanding food and water! But Fire Chief Johnson has forbidden any rescue efforts! Any disturbance, any shifting of the wreckage, he says, might bring the rest of the building crashing down! Now, here's Tom Miller!'

The TV screen showed a reporter with a microphone standing by the wrecked building.

'Emma Weeks!' shouted the reporter, holding his microphone up to a crack. 'Do you hear me? Are you all right?'

Emma's voice was faint but clear. 'Oh, sure! I'm just great! I hope a building falls

on me every day, you know? C'mon, get me out of here!'

Mrs Lambchop sighed. 'Such an unfortunate tone! She is under great strain, of course.'

'Emma's always like that,' Stanley said.

Half an hour later, while Mrs Lambchop was preparing supper, a siren sounded outside, then died away. Opening the front door, Mr Lambchop saw a Fire Department car at the curb. On the doorstep stood Fire Chief Johnson and a very worried-looking man and woman.

'Mr Lambchop?' said Chief Johnson. 'I'll get right to the point, sir. I reckon you heard about little Emma Weeks, trapped in the Merker wreck? Well, Mr and Mrs

Weeks here, and me, we'd like a word with you folks.'

'Of course!' Mr Lambchop led the visitors into the house and introduced them to Mrs Lambchop and Stanley and Arthur.

'Oh, Mrs Weeks!' Mrs Lambchop cried. 'Your poor daughter! You must be dreadfully worried!'

'We are indeed!' said Mr Weeks. 'But Chief Johnson thinks your Stanley might be able to save Emma!'

'Who, me?' and 'Who, Stanley?' said Stanley and Arthur.

Chief Johnson explained. 'Problem is that if a policeman, or one of my firemen, tries to dig his way in to Emma, the whole rest of the building could crash down on 'em! Too bad we don't have a flat fireman, I was thinking. Flat fella could squeeze through all those narrow openings we know are there, 'cause we hear Emma when she calls. Then I recollected the newspaper story, with a picture of Stanley here. Hit me right away! That boy could maybe wiggle in to Emma!'

For a moment, everyone was silent. Then Mrs Lambchop shook her head.

'It sounds terribly dangerous,' she said. 'I'm sorry, but I must say no.'

'It is a tad risky, ma'am,' said Chief Johnson. 'But we've got to remember the boy is already flat.'

Mrs Weeks sobbed. 'Oh, poor Emma! How are we to save her?'

Mrs Lambchop bit her lip.

Stanley remembered something. 'I was just thinking.' He turned to Mr Lambchop. 'The other night? When I got mad about all the crazy things that keep happening to me? Remember what you said? You said that sometime things happen that nobody can see a reason for, and then afterwards some other thing happens, and all of a sudden it seems like the first thing had a reason after all. Well, I was just thinking that me getting flat again was one crazy thing, and that maybe Emma getting stuck where I'm the only one who can try to save her, that might be the second thing.'

Mr Lambchop nodded, and took Mrs

Lambchop's hand. 'We should be very proud of our son, Harriet.'

Mrs Lambchop thought for a moment. 'Stanley,' she said at last. 'Will you be very, very, careful not to let that enormous building fall on you?'

'Okay. Sure,' Stanley said.

Mrs Lambchop turned to Mr and Mrs Weeks. 'We will allow Stanley to help,' she said. 'He will do his best for Emma.'

'Fine boy we got here! Brave as a lion!' shouted Chief Johnson. 'Now listen up, folks! Mrs Lambchop, you help me get things ready! Then Stanley can go right in after Emma! Got that? Everybody meet us at the Merker Building, thirty minutes from now!'

Chapter Seven

Where Are You, Emma?

In the late afternoon sunlight, at the remains of the old Merker Building, the Lambchops and the Weekses watched Chief Johnson prepare Stanley for his rescue attempt. Flash Tobin, the *Daily Sentinel* photographer, was there too, taking pictures.

Mrs Lambchop had supplied two slices of bread and cheese, each wrapped in plastic, and her grandfather's flat silver cigarette case filled with fizzy grape drink. Chief Johnson taped the bread and cheese packets to Stanley's arms and legs, the cigarette case to his chest, and gave him a small, flat torch.

Then he led Stanley up to a tall crack in the wreckage. 'Emma!' he shouted. 'Fella's coming to help you! When he calls your name, you holler back "Here!" so he knows which way to go. Got that?'

Emma's voice came faintly. 'Yeah, yeah! Hurry up! I'm starving!'

Chief Johnson shook Stanley's hand. 'Get goin', son!'

The evening sunlight glowed warmly on the red bricks of the fallen building as Stanley stepped close to the crack. Mrs

Lambchop waved to him, and Stanley waved back. How handsome he is, she thought. How brave, how tall, how flat!

Stanley took two steps forward and disappeared sideways through the crack.

A moment later they heard his shout. 'Hey! It's really dark in here!'

'Hay is for horses, Stanley!' Mrs Lambchop called back. 'Oh, never mind! Good luck, dear!'

This was a dark greater than any he had ever known. Stanley could almost feel the blackness on his skin. He clicked his torch and edged forward without difficulty, but then the crack narrowed, slowing him. The bread slice on his left leg had scraped something, loosening the tape that held it. Pressing the tape back into place, he wiggled forward until he came to what seemed a dead end, but a little swing of the torch showed cracks branching right and left.

'Emma?' he called.

'Here!'

Her voice came from the right, so he moved along that branch. 'Emma?'

'Yeah, yeah! What?'

'When I say your name, you're supposed to say "Here!"'

'I already did that!'

He followed another crack to the left. 'Emma?'

There was no answer. Stanley managed a few more feet and then, quite suddenly, the crack widened. He called again. 'Emma?'

'Bananas!'

'Keep talking,' he shouted. 'I need to hear you!'

'Bananas! Here! Blah, blah! Whatever! Hey, I can see your light!'

And there she was. The crack had widened to become a small cave, at the back of which sat Emma. Her jeans and shirt were smudged with dirt, but it was most surely Emma, squinting against the brightness of his light.

'You!' she exclaimed. 'From school! The flattie!'

Don't lose your temper, Stanley told himself. 'I was the only one they thought could get in here. How are you doing, Emma?'

Emma rolled her eyes. 'Oh, just great! A whole building falls on me, and they send in a flattie! And now I'm starving to death!'

Stanley untaped the slices of bread and cheese, and handed them over.

'Cheese, huh?' Emma put her sandwich together and took a bite. 'I hate cheese. Got anything to drink, flattie?'

'Please don't call me flattie. Here.' He held out the silver cigarette case.

Emma rolled her eyes again. 'I'm not allowed to smoke.'

'It's fizzy drink.'

She opened the cigarette case and sipped. 'Blaahh! I hate grape!'

Chief Johnson's voice rose from a hole in the wall behind her. 'Stanley? You there yet?'

Emma jerked a thumb at the hole. 'It's for you, flattie.'

'I'm here, Chief!' Stanley called. 'Emma's okay.'

He heard cheering, and then the Chief's voice came again. 'See a way out, Stan?'

'I haven't had a chance to look around yet. Emma's eating.'

'We'll wait. Over and out, Stan!'

'You too!' Stanley called.

He waited until Emma had finished her sandwich. 'Emma, how did you get into this mess? What made you come in here?'

'I just came over to look,' Emma said. 'And they had all these signs! "Danger! Keep out!" All over the place, even behind in the parking lot. "Keep out! Danger!

Danger!" I really hate that, you know? So there was this door, and it was open, so I went in.' She finished the fizzy grape drink. 'Okay, let's go.'

'Not the way I came in,' Stanley said. 'I could just barely squeeze through. And we have to be careful, because –'

'I know!' Emma interrupted. 'Chief whatshisname kept telling me: "Don't move around! The whole rest of the building might crash down!" So am I suposed to live down here forever?'

'This door you came through,' Stanley said. 'How far did you come to find this sort of cave we're in?'

'Who said anything about far? I just got inside, and there were these crashing noises, and the whole building was shaking, and I fell down right here! The crashing went on forever! I thought I was going to die!'

'Calm down.' An idea came into Stanley's head. 'Just where was this door? Do you remember?'

'Over there somewhere.' Emma pointed into the darkness of a corner behind her.

Stanley swung his light, but saw only what seemed to be a solid wall of splintered boards, rock, and brick.

Emma pointed a bit left, then right. 'Maybe there . . . I don't know! Was I supposed to take pictures or something? What difference does it make?'

'We might be just a little bit inside that

door,' Stanley said. 'And what we want is to be just outside of it.'

Moving closer to the corner, he saw that a jagged piece of wood protruded at waist level. It came out easily when he tugged, followed by loose dirt.

Emma stood beside him. 'Why are you making this mess?'

He poked in the hole with the stick. 'Maybe I'll find —'

Dirt cascaded from the wall, covering his shoes. He saw light now, not just the little circle from his torch, but daylight! Unmistakably daylight!

'Oooohhhh!' said Emma.

Stanley made the hole still larger, and they saw that a door lay on its side across the bottom of the hole, wreckage limiting the opening on both sides. But it was big enough! They would be able to wiggle through! He ran back to the wall from which Chief Johnson's voice had come.

'We're on our way out!' he shouted. 'We'll be at the back, in the courtyard!'

'Got it!' came the Chief's voice. 'Great work!'

Stanley turned to Emma. 'Let's go!'

'I'll get all dirty, silly,' Emma said. 'Maybe we could just –'

'Come ON!'

'Don't yell!' Emma said, but she crawled quickly through the hole with Stanley right behind her.

Hero!

There was much rejoicing in the courtyard. Mrs Lambchop kissed Stanley and Arthur. Mrs Weeks kissed Emma, and then everyone else, even Flash Tobin, who had arrived to take pictures. Mr Lambchop shook hands with Mr Weeks and Chief Johnson, who announced several times that Stanley was a great hero.

Flash Tobin took a group picture of all the Lambchops. 'Need one more,' he said. 'Emma, just you and Stanley. Your hero, right? Saved your life!'

'I could have got out by myself,' Emma said. 'I just didn't know exactly where the door was.' But she went to stand by Stanley.

'Smile!' Flash Tobin took the picture. 'Yes, that's good!' He gave Stanley a cheerful slap on the back, just as Emma's elbow jabbed hard into Stanley's ribs.

'Owww!' Stanley yelled.

Emma grinned. 'That's for you, Mr Hero!'

'Are you crazy? What —' Stanley stopped. Everybody was staring at him. He felt peculiar, as if . . . Yes! He was getting round again!

'Wow!' Emma said. 'How do you do that?'

'Hooray for you, dear!' shouted Mrs Lambchop, and more cries rose from the others in the courtyard. 'Do you see what I see?. . . He's blowing up! . . . Are we crazy or what?'

Flash Tobin aimed his camera again. 'Hold it, kid!'

But he was too late. Before him now stood a smiling Stanley Lambchop, shaped like a regular boy!

Mr Lambchop ran to hug him, and everyone else applauded.

'Thirty years with the Fire Department, and I never saw anything like that!' said Chief Johnson. 'Wouldn't have missed it!'

'I'm really glad,' Stanley said. 'But what made it happen?'

'What Dr Dan said!' shouted Arthur. 'Remember? The Osteo-posteo-whatever!'

'The OBP! The Osteal Balance Point.' Mr Lambchop smiled. 'Yes! The slap on the back from Flash Tobin, and the poke from Emma! That did it!'

A board fell from the tilting roof of the Merker Building, landing in a corner of the courtyard.

'Let's go, folks,' said Chief Johnson.

'We're not safe here!'
Everyone went home.

Fame!

At bedtime the next evening, the Lambchops read again the *Daily Sentinel* they had enjoyed so much at breakfast that morning.

The front page headline read: RUDE GIRL SAVED! FLAT RESCUER REGAINS SHAPE! Beneath that were two Flash Tobin photographs, the

Lambchop family picture, and the one of Stanley and Emma taken just before she poked him in the ribs. Arthur was particularly pleased with the family picture.

'Finally!' he said. 'Not just Stanley! People could have been wondering if he had a brother, you know? Can I have this one?'

'You may,' said Mrs Lambchop. 'I want the one of Stanley with Emma, for my kitchen wall.'

'I don't care about pictures,' Stanley said. 'I just hope I never go back to being flat.'

Mrs Lambchop patted his hand. 'I told Dr Dan of your recovery, dear. He thinks it most unlikely the flatness will occur again.'

'Yay!' said Stanley.

FLAT STANLEY

by Jeff Brown
Pictures by Scott Nash

EGMONT

Flat Stanley
For J.C. and Tony

Stanley, Flat Again!
For Peter and Wendy, Ozinger, Betsy and Ash

EGMONT

We bring stories to life

Flat Stanley first published in Great Britain 1968
Stanley, Flat Again! first published in Great Britain 2003
This edition published 2005
by Egmont UK Limited
239 Kensington High Street, London W8 6SA

ISBN 1 4052 2321 9

1 3 5 7 9 10 8 6 4 2

A CIP catalogue record for this title is available from the British Library

Printed and bound in Great Britain by the CPI Group

CONTENTS

1. The Big Bulletin Board   1

2. Being Flat   9

3. Stanley the Kite   23

4. The Museum Thieves   35

5. Arthur's Good Idea   55

The Big Bulletin Board

Breakfast was ready.

'I will go and wake the boys,' Mrs Lambchop said to her husband, George Lambchop. Just then their younger son, Arthur, called from the bedroom he shared with his brother Stanley.

'Hey! Come and look! Hey!'

Mr and Mrs Lambchop were both very much in favour of politeness and careful

speech. 'Hay is for horses, Arthur, not people,' Mr Lambchop said as they entered the bedroom. 'Try to remember that.'

'Excuse me,' Arthur said. 'But look!'

He pointed to Stanley's bed. Across it lay the enormous bulletin board that Mr Lambchop had given the boys a Christmas ago, so that they could pin up pictures and messages and maps. It had fallen, during the night, on top of Stanley.

But Stanley was not hurt. In fact he would still have been sleeping if he had not been woken by his brother's shout.

'What's going on here?' he called out cheerfully from beneath the enormous board.

Mr and Mrs Lambchop hurried to lift it from the bed.

'Heavens!' said Mrs Lambchop.

'Gosh!' said Arthur. 'Stanley's flat!'

'As a pancake,' said Mr Lambchop. 'Darndest thing I've ever seen.'

'Let's all have breakfast,' Mrs Lambchop said. 'Then Stanley and I will go and see Doctor Dan and hear what he has to say.'

The examination was almost over.

'How do you feel?' Doctor Dan asked. 'Does it hurt very much?'

'I felt sort of tickly for a while after I got up,' Stanley Lambchop said, 'but I feel fine now.'

'Well, that's mostly how it is with these cases,' said Doctor Dan.

'We'll just have to keep an eye on this young fellow,' he said when he had finished

the examination. 'Sometimes we doctors, despite all our years of training and experience, can only marvel at how little we really know.'

Mrs Lambchop said she thought that Stanley's clothes would have to be altered by

the tailor now, so Doctor Dan told his nurse
to take Stanley's measurements.

Mrs Lambchop wrote them down.

Stanley was four feet tall, about a foot
wide, and half an inch thick.

Being Flat

When Stanley got used to being flat, he enjoyed it.

He could go in and out of rooms, even when the door was closed, just by lying down and sliding through the crack at the bottom.

Mr and Mrs Lambchop said it was silly, but they were quite proud of him.

Arthur got jealous and tried to slide under

a door, but he just banged his head.

Being flat could also be helpful, Stanley found.

He was taking a walk with Mrs Lambchop one afternoon when her favourite ring fell from her finger. The ring rolled across the pavement and down between the bars of a grating that covered a dark, deep shaft. Mrs Lambchop began to cry.

'I have an idea,' Stanley said.

He took the laces out of his shoes and an extra pair out of his pocket and tied them all together to make one long lace. Then he tied the end of that to the back of his belt and gave the other end to his mother.

'Lower me,' he said, 'and I will look for the ring.'

'Thank you, Stanley,' Mrs Lambchop said.

She lowered him between the bars and moved him carefully up and down and from side to side, so that he could search the whole floor of the shaft.

Two policemen came by and stared at Mrs Lambchop as she stood holding the long lace that ran down through the grating. She pretended not to notice them.

'What's the matter, lady?' the first policeman asked. 'Is your yo-yo stuck?'

'I am not playing with a yo-yo!' Mrs Lambchop said sharply. 'My son is at the other end of this lace, if you must know.'

'Get the net, Harry,' said the second policeman. 'We have caught a cuckoo!'

Just then, down in the shaft, Stanley cried out, 'Hooray!'

Mrs Lambchop pulled him up and saw

that he had the ring.

'Good for you, Stanley,' she said. Then she turned angrily to the policemen.

'A cuckoo, indeed!' she said. 'Shame!'

The policemen apologised. 'We didn't get it, lady,' they said. 'We have been hasty. We

see that now.'

'People should think twice before making rude remarks,' said Mrs Lambchop. 'And then not make them at all.'

The policemen realised that was a good rule and said they would try to remember it.

★ ★ ★

One day Stanley got a letter from his friend Thomas Anthony Jeffrey, whose family had moved recently to California. A school holiday was about to begin and Stanley was invited to spend it with the Jeffreys.

'Oh, boy!' Stanley said. 'I would love to go!'

Mr Lambchop sighed. 'A round trip train or aeroplane ticket to California is very expensive,' he said. 'I shall have to think of some cheaper way.'

When Mr Lambchop came home from the office that evening, he brought with him an enormous brown-paper envelope.

'Now then, Stanley,' he said. 'Try this for size.'

The envelope fitted Stanley very well.

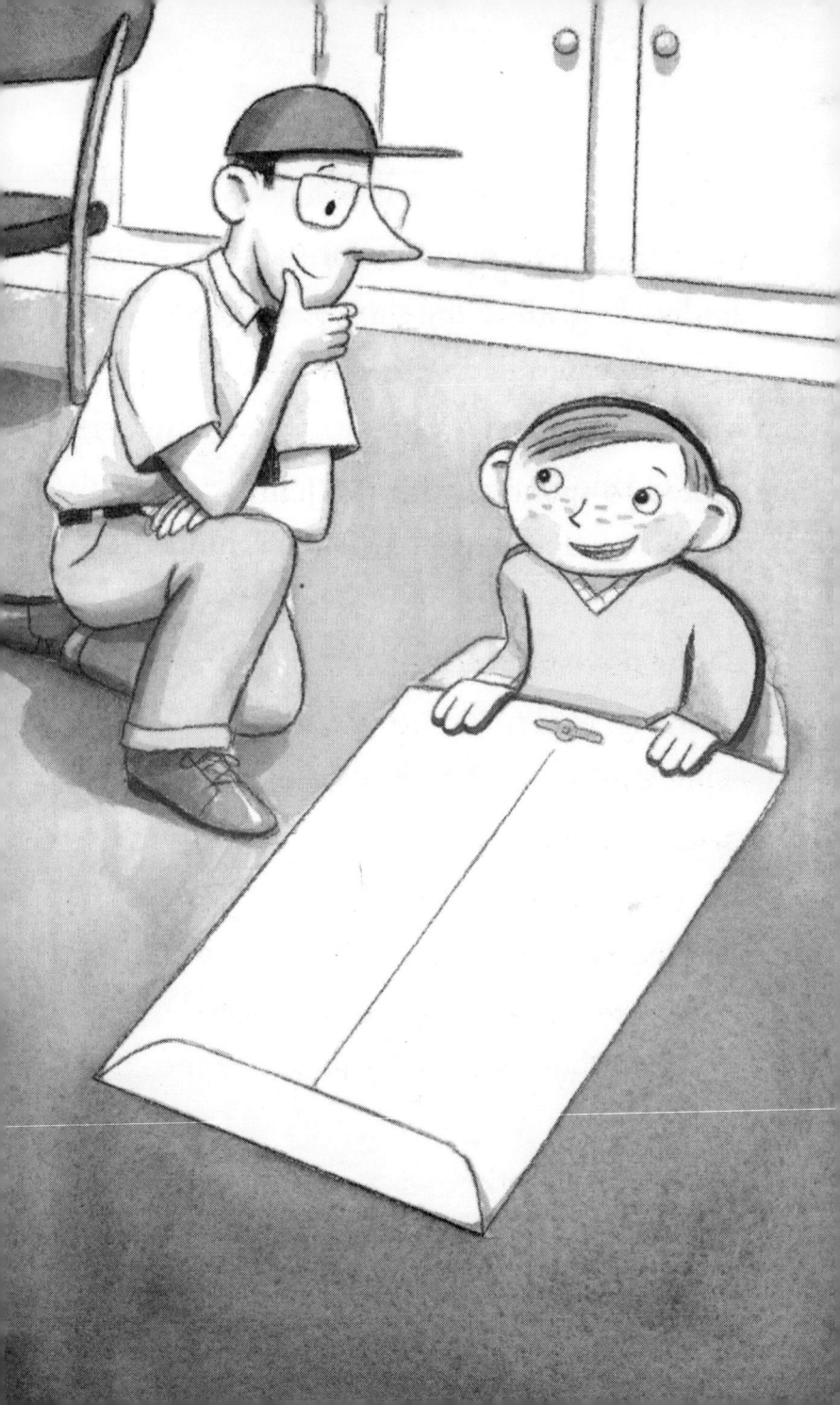

There was even room left over, Mrs Lambchop discovered, for an egg-salad sandwich made with thin bread, and a flat cigarette case filled with milk.

They had to put a great many stamps on the envelope to pay for both airmail and insurance, but it was still much less expensive than a train or aeroplane ticket to California would have been.

The next day Mr and Mrs Lambchop slid Stanley into his envelope, along with the egg-salad sandwich and the cigarette case full of milk, and mailed him from the box on the corner. The envelope had to be folded to fit through the slot, but Stanley was a limber boy and inside the box he straightened up again.

Mrs Lambchop was nervous because

Stanley had never been away from home alone before. She rapped on the box.

'Can you hear me, dear?' she called. 'Are you all right?'

Stanley's voice came quite clearly. 'I'm fine. Can I eat my sandwich now?'

'Wait an hour. And try not to get overheated, dear,' Mrs Lambchop said. Then she and Mr Lambchop cried out 'Good-bye, good-bye!' and went home.

Stanley had a fine time in California. When the visit was over, the Jeffreys returned him in a beautiful white envelope they had made themselves. It had red-and-blue markings to show that it was airmail, and Thomas Jeffrey had lettered it 'Valuable' and 'Fragile' and 'This End Up' on both sides.

Back home Stanley told his family that he had been handled so carefully he never felt a single bump. Mr Lambchop said it proved that jet planes were wonderful, and so was the Post Office Department, and that this was a great age in which to live.

Stanley thought so too.

Stanley the Kite

Mr Lambchop had always liked to take the boys off with him on Sunday afternoons to a museum or roller-skating in the park, but it was difficult when they were crossing streets or moving about in crowds. Stanley and Arthur would often be jostled from his side and Mr Lambchop worried about speeding taxis or that hurrying people might accidentally knock them down.

It was easier after Stanley got flat.

Mr Lambchop discovered that he could roll Stanley up without hurting him at all. He would tie a piece of string around Stanley to keep him from unrolling and make a little loop in the string for himself. It was as simple as carrying a parcel, and he could hold on to Arthur with the other hand.

Stanley did not mind being carried because he had never much liked to walk. Arthur didn't like walking either, but he had to. It made him mad.

One Sunday afternoon, in the street, they met an old college friend of

Mr Lambchop's, a man he had not seen for years.

'Well, George, I see you have bought some wallpaper,' the man said. 'Going to decorate your house, I suppose?'

'Wallpaper?' said Mr Lambchop. 'Oh, no. This is my son Stanley.'

He undid the string and Stanley unrolled.

'How do you do?' Stanley said.

'Nice to meet you, young feller,' the man said. He said to Mr Lambchop, 'George, that boy is flat.'

'Smart, too,' Mr Lambchop said. 'Stanley is third from the top in his class at school.'

'Phooey!' said Arthur.

'This is my younger son, Arthur,' Mr Lambchop said. 'And he will apologise for his rudeness.'

Arthur could only blush and apologise.

Mr Lambchop rolled Stanley up again and they set out for home. It rained quite hard while they were on the way. Stanley, of course, hardly got wet at all, just around the edges, but Arthur got soaked.

Late that night Mr and Mrs Lambchop heard a noise out in the living room. They found Arthur lying on the floor near the bookcase. He had piled a great many volumes of the *Encyclopaedia Britannica* on top of himself.

'Put some more on me,' Arthur said when he saw them. 'Don't just stand there. Help me.'

Mr and Mrs Lambchop sent him back to bed, but the next morning they spoke to Stanley. 'Arthur can't help being jealous,'

they said. 'Be nice to him. You're his big brother, after all.'

Stanley and Arthur were in the park. The day was sunny, but windy too, and many older boys were flying beautiful, enormous kites with long tails, made in all the colours of the rainbow.

Arthur sighed. 'Some day,' he said, 'I will have a big kite and I will win a kite-flying contest and be famous like everyone else. *Nobody* knows who I am these days.'

Stanley remembered what his parents had said. He went to a boy whose kite was broken and borrowed a large spool of string.

'You can fly me, Arthur,' he said. 'Come on.'

He attached the string to himself and gave Arthur the spool to hold. He ran lightly

across the grass, sideways to get up speed, and then he turned to meet the breeze.

Up, up, up . . . UP! went Stanley, being a kite.

He knew just how to manage on the gusts of wind. He faced full into the wind if he wanted to rise, and let it take him from behind when he wanted speed. He had only to turn his thin edge to the wind, carefully, a little at a time, so that it did not hold him, and then he would slip gracefully down towards the earth again.

Arthur let out all the string and Stanley soared high above the trees, a beautiful sight in his pale sweater and bright brown trousers, against the pale-blue sky.

Everyone in the park stood still to watch.

Stanley swooped right and then left in

long, matched swoops. He held his arms by his sides and zoomed at the ground like a rocket and curved up again towards the sun. He sideslipped and circled, and made figure eights and crosses and a star.

Nobody has ever flown the way Stanley Lambchop flew that day. Probably no one ever will again.

After a while, of course, people grew tired of watching and Arthur got tired of running about with the empty spool. Stanley went right on though, showing off.

Three boys came up to Arthur and invited him to join them for a hot dog and some soda pop. Arthur left the spool wedged in the fork of a tree. He did not notice, while

he was eating the hot dog, that the wind was blowing the string and tangling it about the tree.

The string got shorter and shorter, but Stanley did not realise how low he was until leaves brushed his feet, and then it was too late. He got stuck in the branches. Fifteen minutes passed before Arthur and the other boys heard his cries and climbed up to set him free.

Stanley would not speak to his brother that evening, and at bedtime, even though Arthur had apologised, he was still cross.

Alone with Mr Lambchop in the living room, Mrs Lambchop sighed and shook her head. 'You're at the office all day, having fun,' she said. 'You don't realise what I go through with the boys. They're very difficult.'

'Kids are like that,' Mr Lambchop said. 'Phases. Be patient, dear.'

The Museum Thieves

Mr and Mrs O. J. Dart lived in the flat just above the Lambchops. Mr Dart was an important man, the director of a Famous Museum of Art in the city.

Stanley Lambchop had noticed in the lift that Mr Dart, who was ordinarily a cheerful man, had become quite gloomy, but he had no idea what the reason was. And then at breakfast one morning he heard Mr and

Mrs Lambchop talking about Mr Dart.

'I see,' said Mr Lambchop, reading the paper over his coffee cup, 'that still another painting has been stolen from the Famous Museum. It says here that Mr O. J. Dart, the director, is at his wits' end.'

'Oh, dear! Are the police no help?' Mrs Lambchop asked.

'It seems not,' said Mr Lambchop. 'Listen to what the Chief of Police told the newspaper. "We suspect a gang of sneak thieves. These are the worst kind. They work by sneakery, which makes them very difficult to catch. However, my men and I will keep trying. Meanwhile, I hope people will buy tickets for the Policemen's Ball and not park their cars where signs say don't."'

The next morning Stanley Lambchop heard Mr Dart talking to his wife in the lift.

'These sneak thieves work at night,' Mr Dart said. 'It is very hard for our guards to stay awake when they have been on duty all day. And the Famous Museum is so big we cannot guard every picture at the same time. I fear it is hopeless, hopeless, hopeless!'

Suddenly, as if an electric light bulb had lit up in the air above his head, giving out little shooting lines of excitement, Stanley Lambchop had an idea. He told it to Mr Dart.

'Stanley,' Mr Dart said, 'if your mother will give her permission, I will put you and your plan to work this very night!'

Mrs Lambchop gave her permission. 'But

you will have to take a long nap this afternoon,' she said. 'I won't have you up till all hours unless you do.'

That evening, after a long nap, Stanley went with Mr Dart to the Famous Museum. Mr Dart took him into the main hall, where the biggest and most important paintings were hung. He pointed to a huge painting that showed a bearded man, wearing a

floppy velvet hat, playing a violin for a lady who lay on a couch. There was a half-man, half-horse person standing behind them, and three fat children with wings were flying around above. That, Mr Dart explained, was the most expensive painting in the world!

There was an empty picture frame on the opposite wall. We shall hear more about that later on.

Mr Dart took Stanley into his office and said, 'It is time for you to put on a disguise.'

'I had already thought of that,' Stanley Lambchop said, 'and I brought one. My cowboy suit. It has a red bandanna that I can tie over my face. Nobody will recognise me in a million years.'

'No,' Mr Dart said. 'You will have to wear the disguise I have chosen.'

From a closet he took a white dress with a blue sash, a pair of shiny little pointed shoes, a wide straw hat with a blue band that matched the sash, and a wig and a stick.

The wig was made of blonde hair, long and done in ringlets. The stick was curved at the top and it, too, had a blue ribbon on it.

'In this shepherdess disguise,' Mr Dart said, 'you will look like a painting that belongs in the main hall. We do not have cowboy pictures in the main hall.'

Stanley was so disgusted that he could hardly speak. 'I shall look like a girl, that's what I shall look like,' he said. 'I wish I had never had my idea.'

But he was a good sport, so he put on the disguise.

Back in the main hall Mr Dart helped Stanley climb up into the empty picture frame. Stanley was able to stay in place because Mr Dart had cleverly put four small spikes in the wall, one for each hand and foot.

The frame was a perfect fit. Against the wall, Stanley looked just like a picture.

'Except for one thing,' Mr Dart said. 'Shepherdesses are supposed to look happy. They smile at their sheep and at the sky. You look fierce, not happy, Stanley.'

Stanley tried hard to get a faraway look in his eyes and even to smile a little bit.

Mr Dart stood back a few feet and stared at him for a moment. 'Well,' he said, 'it may not be art, but I know what I like.'

He went off to make sure that certain

other parts of Stanley's plan were being taken care of, and Stanley was left alone.

It was very dark in the main hall. A little bit of moonlight came through the windows, and Stanley could just make out the world's most expensive painting on the opposite wall. He felt as though the bearded man with the violin and the lady on the couch and the half-horse person and the winged children were all waiting, as he was, for something to happen.

Time passed and he got tireder and tireder. Anyone would be tired this late at night, especially if he had to stand in a picture frame balancing on little spikes.

Maybe they won't come, Stanley thought. Maybe the sneak thieves won't come at all.

The moon went behind a cloud and then

the main hall was pitch dark. It seemed to get quieter, too, with the darkness. There was absolutely no sound at all. Stanley felt the hair on the back of his neck prickle beneath the golden curls of the wig.

Cr-eee-eee-k . . .

The creaking sound came from right out in the middle of the main hall and even as he heard it Stanley saw, in the same place, a tiny yellow glow of light!

The creaking came again and the glow got bigger. A trap door had opened in the floor and two men came up through it into the hall!

Stanley understood everything all at once. These must be the sneak thieves! They had a secret trap door entrance into the museum from outside. That was why they had never

been caught. And now, tonight, they were back to steal the most expensive painting in the world!

He kept very still in his picture frame

48

and listened to the sneak thieves.

'This is it, Max,' said the first one. 'This is where we art robbers pull a sensational job whilst the civilised community sleeps.'

'Right, Luther,' said the other man. 'In all this great city there is no one to suspect us.'

Ha, ha! thought Stanley Lambchop. That's what you think!

The sneak thieves put down their lantern and took the world's most expensive painting off the wall.

'What would we do to anyone who tried to capture us, Max?' the first man asked.

'We would kill him. What else?' his friend replied.

That was enough to frighten Stanley, and he was even more frightened when Luther came over and stared at him.

'This sheep girl,' Luther said. 'I thought sheep girls were supposed to smile, Max. This one looks scared.'

Just in time, Stanley managed to get a faraway look in his eyes again and to smile, sort of.

'You're crazy, Luther,' Max said. 'She's smiling. And what a pretty little thing she is, too.'

That made Stanley furious. He waited until the sneak thieves had turned back to the world's most expensive painting, and then he shouted in his loudest, most terrifying voice: 'POLICE! POLICE! MR DART! THE SNEAK THIEVES ARE HERE!'

The sneak thieves looked at each other. 'Max,' said the first one, very quietly, 'I think

I heard the sheep girl yell.'

'I think I did too,' said Max in a quivery voice. 'Oh, boy! Yelling pictures. We both need a rest.'

'You'll get a rest, all right!' shouted Mr Dart, rushing in with the Chief of Police and lots of guards and policemen behind him. 'You'll get *arrested*, that's what! Ha, ha, ha!'

The sneak thieves

were too mixed up by Mr Dart's joke and too frightened by the policemen to put up a fight. Before they knew it, they had been handcuffed and led away to jail.

The next morning in the office of the Chief of Police Stanley Lambchop got a medal. The day after that his picture was in all the newspapers.

Arthur's Good Idea

For a while Stanley Lambchop was a famous name. Everywhere that Stanley went, people stared and pointed at him. He could hear them whisper, 'Over there, Harriet, over there! That must be Stanley Lambchop, the one who caught the sneak thieves . . .' and things like that.

But after a few weeks the whispering and the staring stopped. People had other things

to think about. Stanley did not mind. Being famous had been fun, but enough was enough.

And then came a further change, and it was not a pleasant one. People began to laugh and make fun of him as he passed by. 'Hello, Super-Skinny!' they would shout, and even ruder things, about the way he looked.

Stanley told his parents how he felt. 'It's the other kids I mostly mind,' he said. 'They don't like me any more because I'm different. Flat.'

'Shame on them,' Mrs Lambchop said. 'It is wrong to dislike people for their shapes. Or their religion, for that matter, or the colour of their skin.'

'I know,' Stanley said. 'Only maybe it's

impossible for everybody to like *everybody*.'

'Perhaps,' said Mrs Lambchop. 'But they can try.'

Later that night Arthur Lambchop was woken by the sound of crying. In the darkness he crept across the room and knelt by Stanley's bed.

'Are you okay?' he said.

'Go away,' Stanley said.

'Don't be mad at me,' Arthur said. 'You're still mad because I let you get tangled the day you were my kite, I guess.'

'Skip it, will you?' Stanley said. 'I'm not mad. Go away.'

'Please let's be friends . . .' Arthur couldn't help crying a little, too. 'Oh, Stanley,' he said. 'Please tell me what's wrong?'

Stanley waited for a long time before he

spoke. 'The thing is,' he said, 'I'm just not happy any more. I'm tired of being flat. I want to be a proper shape again, like other people. But I'll have to go on being flat for ever. It makes me sick.'

'Oh, Stanley,' Arthur said. He dried his tears on a corner of Stanley's sheet and could think of nothing more to say.

'Don't talk about what I just said,' Stanley told him. 'I don't want the folks to worry. That would only make it worse.'

'You're brave,' Arthur said. 'You really are.'

He took hold of Stanley's hand. The two brothers sat together in the darkness, being friends. They were both still sad, but each one felt a *little* better than he had before.

And then, suddenly, though he was not even trying to think, Arthur had an idea.

He jumped up and turned on the light and ran to the big storage box where toys and things were kept. He began to rummage in the box.

Stanley sat up in bed to watch.

Arthur flung aside a football and some lead soldiers and aeroplane models and lots of wooden blocks, and then he said, 'Aha!' He had found what he wanted – an old bicycle pump. He held it up, and Stanley and he looked at each other.

'Okay,' Stanley said at last. 'But take it easy.' He put the end of the long pump hose in his mouth and clamped his lips tightly about it so that no air could escape.

'I'll go slowly,' Arthur said. 'If it hurts or anything, wiggle your hand at me.'

He began to pump. At first nothing

happened except that Stanley's cheeks bulged a bit. Arthur watched his hand, but there was no wiggle signal, so he pumped on. Then, suddenly, Stanley's top half began to swell.

'It's working! It's working!' shouted Arthur, pumping away.

Stanley spread his arms so that the air could get round inside him more easily. He got bigger and bigger. The buttons of his pyjama top burst off – *Pop! Pop! Pop!* A moment more and he was all rounded out: head and body, arms and legs. But not his right foot. That foot stayed flat.

Arthur stopped pumping. 'It's like trying to do the very last bit of those long balloons,' he said. 'Maybe a shake would help.'

Stanley shook his right foot twice, and

with a little *whooshing* sound it swelled out to match the left one. There stood Stanley Lambchop as he used to be, as if he had never been flat at all!

'Thank you, Arthur,' Stanley said. 'Thank you very much.'

The brothers were shaking hands when Mr Lambchop strode into the room with Mrs Lambchop right behind him. 'We heard you!' said Mr Lambchop. 'Up and talking when you ought to be asleep, eh? Shame on –'

'GEORGE!' said Mrs Lambchop. 'Stanley's *round* again!'

'You're right!' said Mr Lambchop, noticing. 'Good for you, Stanley!'

'I'm the one who did it,' Arthur said. 'I blew him up.'

Everyone was terribly excited and happy, of course. Mrs Lambchop made hot chocolate to celebrate the occasion, and several toasts were drunk to Arthur for his cleverness.

When the little party was over, Mr and Mrs Lambchop tucked the boys back into their beds and kissed them, and then they turned out the light. 'Good night,' they said.

'Good night,' said Stanley and Arthur.

It had been a long and tiring day. Very soon all the Lambchops were asleep.

The End

Arthur cut the family picture out of the paper, and used a red pencil to draw an arrow, pointing up at him, in the white space at the bottom. Under the arrow, he wrote, *Hero's Brother*! Then he taped the picture to the wall above his bed.

Soon all the Lambchops were asleep.

The End